D1271015

SAMANTHA CARDIGAN
and the *Ghastly Twirling Sickness*

INTERNATIONAL
ADVENTURERS

DAVID SUTHERLAND   DAVID ROBERTS

To Camilla
D.S.

For Thea
D.R.

Crabtree Publishing Company
www.crabtreebooks.com

PMB 16A, 350 Fifth Avenue,
Suite 3308,
New York, NY 10118

616 Welland Avenue,
St. Catharines, Ontario
Canada, L2M 5V6

Sutherland, David, 1956-
  Samantha Cardigan and the ghastly twirling sickness / David
Sutherland ; illustrated by David Roberts. p. cm. -- (Red bananas)
  Summary: When a strange twirling sickness grips the kingdom of Nedakh, its
Emperor calls on international adventurers Samantha Cardigan and Rabbit to
untangle the mystery.
  ISBN-13: 978-0-7787-1069-1 (rlb) -- ISBN-10: 0-7787-1069-6 (rlb)
  ISBN-13: 978-0-7787-1085-1 (pbk) -- ISBN-10: 0-7787-1085-8 (pbk)
  [1. Rabbits--Fiction. 2. Emperors--Fiction. 3. Adventure and adventurers--
Fiction.] I. Roberts, David, 1970- ill. II. Title. III. Series.
  PZ7.S966743Sam 2005
  [Fic]--dc22   2005001568 LC

Published by Crabtree Publishing in 2005
First published in 2003 by Egmont Books Ltd.
Text copyright © David Sutherland 2003
Illustrations © David Roberts 2003
The Author and Illustrator have asserted their moral rights.
Paperback ISBN 0-7787-1085-8
Reinforced Hardcover Binding ISBN 0-7787-1069-6

1 2 3 4 5 6 7 8 9 0 Printed in Italy 4 3 2 1 0 9 8 7 6 5

Contents

Red Bananas

In the Palace of the Seven Moons

The tiniest slip could have been fatal!
Samantha Cardigan and Rabbit,
International Adventurers, clung to the rock
face and edged along the footpath. It was
extremely dangerous, but it was the only way
to reach the mountain kingdom of Nedakh.

Slowly, they made their way down into
a peaceful valley. In the middle of a rice
paddy, a man with a broad-brimmed
hat was twirling around and around.
"How odd," thought
Samantha Cardigan.

Later, they passed
a straw-roofed cottage. In
the yard, a woman was spinning
in circles, surrounded by chickens.
The chickens did not know what to
make of it. Neither did Samantha Cardigan.
"Maybe it's a sort of dance," she thought
and hurried on her way.

7

They walked all morning and finally arrived at the Palace of the Seven Moons. They were immediately ushered into the Great Hall for their meeting with the Emperor. He sat on a cushion surrounded by his advisers.

"I trust your journey was not too difficult?" he asked. "Tell me, did you see anything unusual along the way?"

"Um, not really," replied Samantha. "Why do you ask?"

The Emperor sighed. "My land is gripped by a terrible plague. Day by day it spreads . . ."

"That's terrible news!"

"We are suffering from a terrible outbreak of Ghastly Twirling Sickness."

"*Ghastly Twirling Sickness?*"

"It started a month ago. Our bakers make no bread.

Farmers grow no rice.

Goats go unmilked. We sent for you at once, of course."

Samantha Cardigan had never heard of Ghastly Twirling Sickness before.

"What do you think of this, Rabbit?"

I feel sick!

10

But before Rabbit could answer, a large man with bushy sideburns stepped forward.

"I am Doctor Inchbutt. It is a well known medical fact that Ghastly Twirling Sickness is a simple disorder of the *confabula fibula*. The cure is also well known. The patient must soak for three days in a tub of dog slobber."

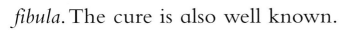

"Well, if you know the remedy, why haven't you cured anyone?" asked Samantha.

"Hmm . . . can't get enough dog slobber. Takes a lot to fill a tub, you know."

Just then, Rabbit whispered something in Samantha Cardigan's ear. She screwed up her face in disbelief.

"Why should you be interested in a blind donkey with three stars on its leg?" she blurted out. "What are you talking about? Can't you see we're in the middle of something important?"

The Emperor's advisers gave her a very funny look, especially Doctor Inchbutt. They weren't used to discussing matters of national importance with a rabbit.

Samantha Cardigan went red in the face
and started babbling. "Well, we'd better take
a look around and see what we can see!
Er, nice to meet you!"

Then she grabbed Rabbit by the arm and
rushed out of the Great Hall.

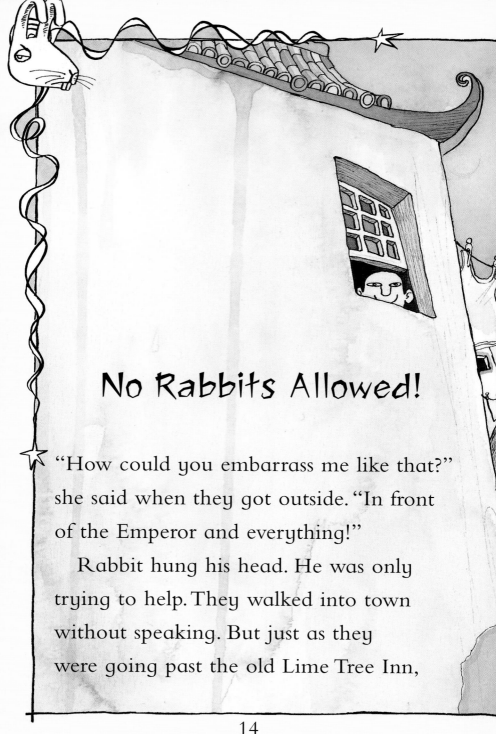

No Rabbits Allowed!

"How could you embarrass me like that?" she said when they got outside. "In front of the Emperor and everything!"

Rabbit hung his head. He was only trying to help. They walked into town without speaking. But just as they were going past the old Lime Tree Inn,

Samantha Cardigan stopped in her tracks.
Tied to the railing was a blind donkey. It
had three stars branded on its left hind leg.

She was very surprised. Rabbit whispered something else in her ear.

"OK, I'll ask inside, but this had better be good!"

Climbing the steps, she pushed open the front door and went inside. Behind the desk, an old woman was asleep in a leather chair.

"Excuse me," said Samantha Cardigan loudly. "I would like to speak to the owner of that blind donkey."

The woman awoke
with a start.

"Go away!" she demanded.
"No rabbits allowed!
We're full up. In fact,
we're closed."

Samantha Cardigan
was quite taken aback.

"There's no need to
be so rude," she said.
"How can you
be closed if you're
full up? Besides I don't
want a room. I just want
to speak to the . . ."

We're FULL.

VACANCIES

"He doesn't want to speak to anyone.
In fact, he's not even staying here. I said
that already. We're completely empty.
Away you go now. No rabbits allowed!"

The old woman took her guests by the arm, and a moment later, they were back on the front steps with the big door closing behind them.

"Well, something funny is going on here, that's for sure!" said Samantha Cardigan. Out of the corner of her eye, she spied a hairy face huffing and puffing along the street.

What's he doing here?

Hmm.

"Look," she exclaimed. "That's Doctor Inchbutt!"

Quickly they hid around the corner. The doctor marched up the front steps, checking over his shoulder to see if he had been followed. He opened the door and disappeared inside.

Samantha Cardigan and Rabbit crept
down the alley to the back of the building.
Silently, they tiptoed up the rickety fire
escape, listening outside each window. On the

third floor, they heard
muffled voices . . .

Putting her eye up
to the grimy window,
Samantha Cardigan
peered inside.

Doctor Inchbutt

was there, wringing his hands and looking
very nervous. Another man was sitting in
an armchair. From the side, all she could
see was the top of his dark blue hood.

Your
Greatness.

Suddenly, the hooded man leapt up and hissed, "Everything must be ready by tonight. At midnight in the old quarry!"

With that, he flung a wad of money at the big man's feet. Scooping it up, the doctor scuttled out of the room backward, nodding and bowing.

Samantha Cardigan and Rabbit turned away from the window. They crept down the fire escape and quickly walked away from the Lime Tree Inn.

A Hair From
Every Head

What on earth was the doctor up to? Who was that hooded man? What was going to happen at midnight in the old quarry? There was only one way to find out . . .

With these thoughts tumbling around in her head, Rabbit whispered something else in Samantha Cardigan's ear. She realized then that he had gone completely crazy.

"A vacuum cleaner?" she demanded.

"Have you gone out of your rabbitty little mind? The entire kingdom is gripped by Ghastly Twirling Sickness, Doctor Inchbutt is up to something terrible, and you want to buy a vacuum cleaner!"

But before she could stop him, Rabbit scampered into the nearest store and came back with a large box.

LIGHTWEIGHT, BATTERY-POWERED INFLATABLE VACUUM CLEANER, IDEAL FOR TRAVELING!

Samantha Cardigan shook her head. Rabbit did the silliest things sometimes! She stuffed the box into her backpack and they made their way back to the Palace of the Seven Moons to report to the Emperor. They found him alone with Doctor Inchbutt.

"Ah, Miss Cardigan," the doctor sneered. "Did you learn anything interesting in town?"

"Well, not really," she lied.

"Hmm," the fat man grunted. "We can't expect too much. You're only a girl, after all.

"I was just explaining to His Majesty how we might develop a vaccination. For that we need to collect a hair from every person's head. Now, Your Highness, if I may be so bold . . ."

Got you!

Oow!

The doctor leaned over and plucked a hair from the Emperor's head. Then he turned to Samantha Cardigan.

"I'll need one from you as well, of course, for your own protection."

Samantha Cardigan took a step back.
She knew he was up to no good, but what
could she say? She had no proof! Before
she could say anything, the doctor snatched
a hair from her head.

"I'll just get these off to the lab then,"
he sang cheerily.

As soon as he was out of the room, Samantha Cardigan cried out, "Your Majesty, something truly awful is happening!"

"I am well aware of that. That's why we sent for you!"

"Well, yes, but it's Doctor Inchbutt! He's, he's . . ."

"Ah, yes," the old man interrupted. "He's wonderful, isn't he? We are so lucky to have him. Now, if you will excuse me, I am expecting the Queen of Peru."

Royal duties, you know.

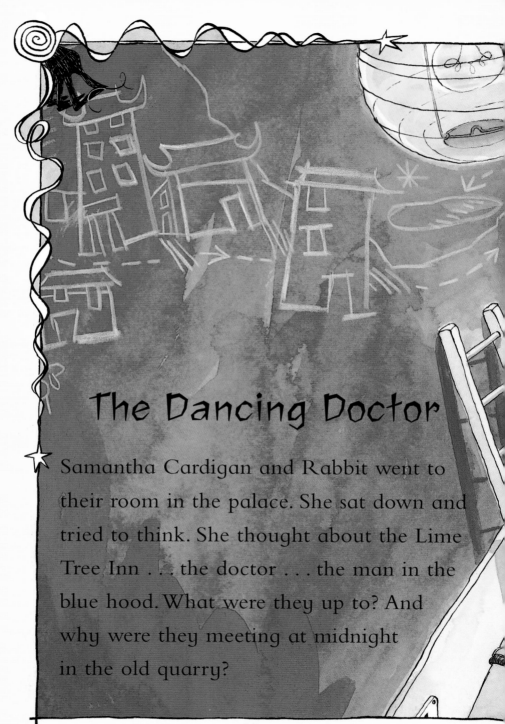

The Dancing Doctor

Samantha Cardigan and Rabbit went to their room in the palace. She sat down and tried to think. She thought about the Lime Tree Inn . . . the doctor . . . the man in the blue hood. What were they up to? And why were they meeting at midnight in the old quarry?

A servant boy came to the door with
a big bowl of chips and some carrots.

Samantha Cardigan asked if he knew
the way to the old quarry.

He explained the directions in great detail.

Samantha Cardigan thanked him and took the carrots to Rabbit. She lay down on the bed, eating her chips. It had been such a tiring day. She decided to close her eyes, just for five minutes . . .

Just a quick nap.

Look at the time, Rabbit!

She fell fast asleep, of course. Rabbit woke her up four hours later. She looked at her watch. "Oh, my goodness. A quarter to twelve!"

They rushed out of the palace . . .

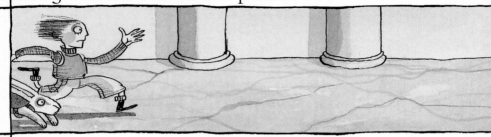

across a courtyard . . .

past some stables . . .

over a wooden gate, and into a lemon grove.
Dashing through the trees, they came out
into a narrow path. It led up a hill and soon
they could see out over the quarry.

They clambered
down some rocky
steps to the bottom.
Just up ahead, they
could hear voices.
Carefully, they
peered out from
behind a boulder.

"I have all the hairs you need," Doctor
Inchbutt was saying. "From the Emperor,
his advisers, and that meddlesome
Samantha Cardigan."

"Show me," ordered the man in the
blue hood.

The doctor handed over a small package.
The hooded man opened it and held up
a few strands.

"Excellent! Now I can cast my dancing spell over the entire palace. No one will be able to stop me!"

"Hmm . . . no one, that's for sure." The doctor nodded and bowed. "Now, if we could just settle the rest of my fee?"

"Your fee . . . of course!"

With that, the hooded man snatched a hair from the doctor's own head! Muttering an ancient spell, he twirled it between his fingers and threw it into the air. Instantly, the big man began to jerk and twitch and soon he was spinning around and around!

Aargh!

The Empty Cloak

That was when Rabbit decided to get out his inflatable vacuum cleaner.

"What do you think you're doing, you crazy rabbit?" Samantha Cardigan hissed. "This is no time for cleaning!"

On the other side of the boulder, the hooded man froze.

"Who's that?" he demanded. "Who's there?"

Samantha Cardigan held her breath.

"Well . . . let me see if it is who I think it is!"

Picking a strand from his bundle of hairs, he held it up and twirled it between his fingers . . .

Unable to resist, Samantha Cardigan jerked to her feet and pirouetted out from her hiding place.

In a trance, she joined the doctor in a whirling, twirling dance.

A hideous peel of laughter came from deep inside the blue hood. The man threw back his head and let his cloak fall to the ground. But . . . there was no man inside it! Only a wispy, ghostly form with glowing, red eyes.

Away he flew around the quarry, laughing
and shrieking, weaving in between his
dancing victims.

Meanwhile, Rabbit finished blowing up
his inflatable vacuum cleaner. He waited for
the wizard to come into range. He held up
the end of the hose. He flicked the switch . . .

But nothing happened. He'd forgotten to
put the batteries in!

Desperately Rabbit fumbled with the
batteries, while the evil Guul made a wide
turn and came whizzing back towards
him. But in his panic, he dropped them!

Guul's terrible eyes bore down on
him in the dark, burning
with fury.

39

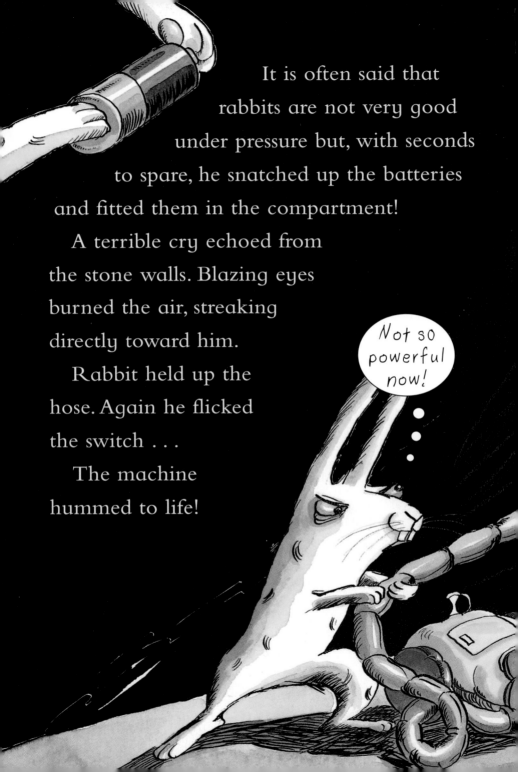

It is often said that rabbits are not very good under pressure but, with seconds to spare, he snatched up the batteries and fitted them in the compartment!

A terrible cry echoed from the stone walls. Blazing eyes burned the air, streaking directly toward him.

Rabbit held up the hose. Again he flicked the switch . . .

The machine hummed to life!

Not so powerful now!

Instantly, the wicked spell was broken.
All over the kingdom, people
stopped twirling.

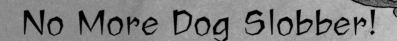

No More Dog Slobber!

The following day, at the Palace of the Seven Moons, Samantha Cardigan told the Emperor the whole story. The old man was astonished to think that his own doctor could have betrayed him.

"Tell me, how did Rabbit suspect it was the wizard Guul?"

"Well, rabbits know a lot of magicians, you see, from being pulled out of so many hats. One of the magicians he worked with told him about a ghostly wizard who rode a blind donkey. His favorite spell was a sort of twirling trance. Luckily for us, his guess was correct."

For her bravery, the Emperor gave Samantha Cardigan a shiny gold medal.

Rabbits, as you know, never wear medals, so he got some lettuce and a bunch of carrots instead.

The inflatable vacuum cleaner with Guul inside was sealed in a metal trunk with seventeen locks. And Doctor Inchbutt was left to soak in a tub of dog slobber, which was exactly where he belonged!

Then Samantha Cardigan and Rabbit, International Adventurers, waved goodbye to the Emperor. Just as they were leaving the palace, a man arrived with an urgent telegram. Samantha Cardigan read it with excitement.

"Come, Rabbit," she cried, "we're off to the Sahara Desert!"

HPARX   +
        SUTHE

SUTHERLAND, DAVID
   SAMANTHA CARDIGAN
   AND THE GHASTLY...
PARK PLACE
11/05